Meant

To Be

A Novel

By:

Tonya L.

Lambert

ISBN978-0-6152-0809-1

Meant to Be

 A novel

Written by Tonya L Lambert

Copyright 2007

ISBN: 978-0-6152-0809-1

Published by Lock and Key to My Heart Publishing, 2008.

Edited by Anthony Ackerley and Melissa Dear.

The Author would like to thank them and everyone else in her life who has supported her and made this book possible.

About the author:

Tonya L. Lambert is the mother of three beautiful daughters and works as a Licensed Practical Nurse and a freelance writer in Virginia. She loves spending time with her family and reading in what little spare time she has. She has published numerous pieces in newspapers and both print and online magazines, from poetry and puzzles to articles, guest editorials and blogs. This is the first book she has published. Look out for her next book which will be a humorous book about the funny side of the nursing profession.

CHAPTER ONE- WISHES AND DREAMS

The beautiful princess sat looking out of her window. She had a wonderful view of the kingdom below from her high lookout. Suddenly, she felt the floor rattling beneath her pink, sparkly slippers.

She looked up from her feet to see a dragon approaching in the distance, setting fire to everything in its path. A trail of scorched trees and houses were in his wake. He had gotten close enough to stomp in the muddy moat surrounding the castle when the princess found her voice and started yelling, "HELP! Somebody save me!"

Just then she saw a gallant prince on his pure white stallion. His hair waved in the wind as he raised his mighty sword. "I'll help you, princess! For you are the most beautiful girl in all the land!"

"My hero!" the princess blushed as the stallion galloped towards the dragon. She watched eagerly as the prince got closer and closer to the beast.

"Anything for you, Princess Annette… Annette… Annette" his voice started fading, getting further and further away.

"Annette! Come down for breakfast before it gets cold! This is your last call!" Annette opened her eyes and rubbed them, trying to remove the sleep that had collected in the corners of them.

"What a dream!" Annette mumbled to herself as she got out of her bed. She hated getting out of the bed. It always seemed so soft and warm right before she had to get out of it. Besides, she wanted to see if the handsome prince would complete his mission and slay the dragon.

Maybe another time, she told herself as she picked out her clothes and went to the bathroom to get ready. It really wasn't that hard to drag herself out of bed, not with the smell of her mother's homemade pancakes wafting down the hall.

"Good morning!" Annette's sister Alisa greeted her cheerfully as she poured syrup over her pancakes.

"Good morning, Alisa. Hey! Don't eat all the syrup!"

Alisa giggled, her eyes lighting up. Annette thought about how cute her little sister was. She had plump, rosy cheeks and freckles across the bridge of her nose. There was a big difference in age between the girls, but they had always been as close any sisters they knew. Annette always looked out for the younger Wilkins girl, like any good big sister should.

"You don't have much longer in school, Annette. Are you getting excited about graduation yet?" her mother asked as she served a plateful of pancakes to her daughter.

"In a way, I am excited, but I'm also a little scared, to be honest with you."

"Don't be scared, sweetheart," her mother tried to reassure her. "I know you will do just great in nursing school. And you know you're welcome to stay here as long as you need to. I don't think I'm ready for you to move out anyway, and neither is your dad."

"Or me!" piped up Alisa.

This brought a smile to Annette's face. She didn't even want to think about leaving her loving family just yet, and she knew they weren't about to push her out of the house. She couldn't understand why some of her friends at school couldn't wait to move out of their parents' houses. Some even wanted to move away from their small town into a bigger city. The thought of doing something like that frightened Annette. Of course many of her friends didn't have a tight-knit family like Annette's. Annette was certainly glad to have been born into the family that she was.

"You girls had better get moving, or you're going to be late for school," her mom's warning broke Annette out of her reverie.

Annette grabbed her books and kissed her mom's cheek before walking out the door. "Bye, mom! I love you!"

Alisa followed closely behind her. Annette always walked Alisa out to her bus stop where she caught the elementary school bus, then Annette walked to the high school which was only a quarter of a mile from their house. She enjoyed the walk each morning. It gave her time to gather her thoughts and get some fresh air before school, and was one of her few opportunities during the day to spend some quiet time by herself. Besides, a little exercise never hurt, especially after her mother's breakfasts.

As she walked, Annette looked around at the serene neighborhood. The houses had plenty of room between them and were separated by gently rolling hills covered with the greenest grass. Annette took a deep breath of cool, clean air and appreciated all of the beauty God had created.

This morning, her mom's question had Annette thinking about her plans for the future. She had been planning for quite some time to go to nursing school after graduation. Math and science had always been her strong subjects in school, and she loved working with people.

Annette had helped take care of her grandmother several years prior when the elderly lady had become too weak from a stroke to take care of herself. The family did not want to put Nana in a nursing home, so everyone pitched in to help, even Annette who was only twelve at the time. Nana stayed in the Wilkins' household for several months before she passed away. Even though it was hard on Annette to watch her grandmother die after taking care of her every day after school, she felt a peace within her heart, knowing that she had done everything she could to help her Nana while she was still alive.

Caring for her Nana made Annette realize that nursing was her true calling. Doing some volunteer work at the local community hospital solidified that decision even more. Annette especially enjoyed visiting with the older patients who didn't have family to come and visit them. She knew this kind of work would fulfill her and make her happy, just like caring for Nana did.

Annette had such fond memories of her long talks with Nana as she stayed with her by her bedside. She would sit in a chair right next to Nana's bed and read to her. Nana liked hearing Annette read so much that Annette would read her anything. She started with get-well cards and letters Nana had received from her friends and family, and then she went on to read the day's newspaper. Sometimes Annette would read

Little House on the Prairie books to her Nana. Annette loved those books and imagined herself living back in those times. The books reminded Nana of her own childhood, and she shared memories with Annette about growing up.

Annette's absolute favorite part of caring for her grandmother was hearing the older lady's stories about times long past. Her favorite story was the one about how her grandparents met and started dating. She listened to the story so many times that she knew it by heart, but she still listened every time as if she had never heard the story before in her life.

"It was a long time ago, over fifty years, when I met your grandfather. We had gone to the schoolhouse together, but we never dated then, although we said hello to each other. We were so young those days, kids left school pretty early to help out at home with younger kids, or go to work to help support the family. It wasn't like today when education is thought of as being most important for someone your age. We saw each other in passing and were friendly enough, but that was it for a while.

I was helping my father out at his shop one day when your grandpa came in to get some fruit. We chatted briefly, but I was working so we couldn't talk much. It was the first time we'd seen each other in a while. Then a few months later, I was visiting some relatives across town. I saw him across the street on a porch when I arrived. He was in the same neighborhood visiting his uncle. I thought that was quite a coincidence, and we laughed about it. It seemed like it wouldn't be much chance of seeing each other that far from home, and we thought it was strange. We couldn't visit much that day either, though, because we were both guests in our family members' houses and we didn't want to be rude.

Finally, I went to the butcher a few blocks from my house one day. It had been several weeks since the last time I'd seen Charles and I thought about him every now and then, and hoped I'd run into him again, but it still caught me off guard when I saw him at the butcher's shop.

He was even more handsome than I remembered. He asked me if he could carry my bag of meat home for me. I told him that would be great, although of course I was capable of carrying it myself, I wanted the chance to talk to him a little bit longer.

I showed him where my house was, and he came in to meet my Pa and asked if he could come calling. My Pa agreed. I was getting to the age where a lot of girls my age were getting married, and my Pa knew him and thought he was a good man.

We ended up courting for a few months before Charles asked my father for my hand in marriage. That's how it was done in those days. I was so happy, I loved Charles dearly. We were married for forty-seven years when he died, and had four children and eleven grandchildren, and I wouldn't trade a second I had with him for anything in the world!

Of course, we had our ups and downs, like any husband and wife do, but we were madly in love with each other. I'm still just as much in love with him now as when we got married, and I can't wait to see him on the other side. I know he's there with God, waiting patiently for me to join him."

The story gave Annette goose bumps every time she heard it, and it filled her eyes with tears even as a young girl. She wondered now if she would be lucky enough to find a love so deep and true. It almost seemed like too much to ask God for, but she still did every night when she prayed before going to bed. He didn't need to ride in on a white stallion to save her from a fire-breathing dragon, but she still asked God to send her the prince that he had made for her, when the time was right.

Of course, she was in no hurry right now, the main things on her mind were her upcoming graduation and getting ready for nursing school. Still, it was fun to think about finding that handsome prince like in the fairy tales her mother read to her from the time she was a little baby. Her mother instilled in Annette that true love really was out there and that there was a special person for her that God would lead her to at the perfect time, when it was meant to be.

Annette had always believed in this and remembered it from the time she was a child rocking on her mother's knee. Now that she was a young woman, she still thought about it from time to time, but she didn't think she should go looking for love. She knew that it would find her, and God would lead her special someone to her, maybe when she least suspected.

CHAPTER TWO- NEW FRIENDS

When Annette arrived at the school, she found her best friend Betty waiting for her beside the schoolhouse door. The two girls walked inside the building, chattering on about what they had done over the weekend. They were both very active in their church, so Betty wanted to know what kind of activities the youth group had done that weekend since she had gone out of town with her mother.

As they walked down the main corridor of the school, Annette noticed an unfamiliar face. It was a tall boy with dark hair struggling with his locker. He had a small slip of paper in one hand with the combination written on it, and a pile of brand-new books at his feet.

"Do you need some help?" Annette asked the boy.

"Sure, that would be great. I've never had much luck with these things", he answered.

Annette showed him the secret to opening the old lockers. "Wow, you're just an old pro at that," he told Annette. "A cute one, too," he added, with a wink.

Annette felt a blush rise to her cheeks and she didn't know what to say, which was unusual for her. "I, uh, um..." she stammered.

The boy laughed. "You're modest, I like that. Although I can't see how you could be. I'm sure guys tell you how cute you are all the time."

"I, um, need to get to class." Annette grabbed Betty's hand and headed towards her first period class before she could embarrass herself any more.

When they were about halfway down the hall, the boy shouted, "Hey, locker pro! Do you have a name?"

Annette cleared her throat, and then shouted her name back to him.

"My name is Joshua. Joshua Burton. I'll see you around, I hope."

"I'll see you at lunch," Annette whispered to Betty as she ducked into her English class.

Betty stood outside the door and watched her friend scurry into the classroom, very preoccupied. Betty shook her head. She'd never seen Annette act this way before. Of course, it's not every day that a good-looking new guy moves to their small town, either.

Betty had never seen Annette get all flustered over boys, that wasn't the kind of girl she was. Betty was definitely the boy-crazy one of the duo. Betty went off to her History class, anxious to see what Annette had to say about Joshua at lunch time.

Annette sat in English class, but her mind was not on her work. It kept drifting back to Joshua. He was tall and seemed to look a little older than high school age. He had the darkest hair, but he had intense, clear blue eyes that just seemed to sparkle.

Joshua, she said the name over in her mind. It was a biblical name. Annette found herself wondering if Joshua was a Christian. He did seem like quite a flirt. Maybe he's just outgoing, she told herself. Maybe he was just trying to be friendly and she was mistaking his openness for flirting because he was so cute.

Annette had been on a few dates, like most seventeen year old girls. Her parents had a strict rule about not dating before the age of sixteen. Annette did feel that was a bit old-fashioned, until she turned sixteen and started to go on dates occasionally.

Most of the boys she went out with weren't Christian and the dates she went on usually ended in one of two ways. She either asked the boy to take her home because she felt pressured and uncomfortable, or the boy would end up acting bored with her talk about God and church. That is why Annette had made a solemn vow to only date Christian boys.

Finding a suitable Christian guy was a hard task in her small town. Most of the boys at her church were either too old for her or too young, it seemed. The few who were around the same age as her had steady girlfriends already or just had a brother-sister type of relationship with Annette, with no romantic sparks between them.

Because of all of this, Annette had put love on the back burner for now. She figured she should concentrate on her school, church, and volunteer work at the hospital anyway. She had never been crazy about a boy before. So why couldn't she take her mind off of a certain dark-haired boy with locker trouble?

Annette tried to shake the thought out of her head. What would be the chances of Joshua being a good, Christian boy, instead of just another one of those boys who was looking for a few dates and a good time? That would be too much to ask for. She forced herself to concentrate on her English work. She didn't need a boy invading her thoughts, not with college only a few short months away.

Annette rushed to the lunch room, to the table where she and Betty usually sat. She spread out her food in front of her and looked around to see if she saw Betty getting into the lunch line. Betty always bought her lunch, while Annette brought her own. She didn't like the school food, which was usually fried and greasy. Betty usually brought a carton of milk or juice for her friend from the line.

"Is this seat taken?" a masculine voice interrupted Annette's train of thought. She looked up to see none other than the boy who had occupied her thoughts all morning long.

"My friend Betty sits with me, but I'm sure she won't care if you sit with us as well." Annette's voice sounded calm, but she was mad at herself for letting a blush creep into her cheeks again. She tried to will the heat out of her face, but doubted it would help.

"Okay, great. I'll get myself some lunch and I'll be right back." Joshua flashed Annette a big, toothy grin as he set down his books, then headed for the lunch line.

Annette let out a great big sigh as soon as Joshua was out of her ear shot. Why was she acting like this? Annette was usually so cool and collected.

"He's pretty cute, huh?" Betty teased, raising and lowering her eyebrows as she covered her mouth to hide a little giggle.

"Betty! I'm so glad you're back. I have GOT to talk to you!"

"Would it be about Mr. Joshua Blue-Eyes?"

"Yes, as a matter of fact, it would be," Annette rolled her eyes. "Betty, why can't I get him off my mind? You know this isn't like me at all!"

"It looks like someone's been bitten by the love bug," Betty sang, and then broke out into giggles again. "It's about time that happened to you. Now, I wonder…do you think he has a cute brother for me?"

"Here he comes, Betty, quiet!"

'I guess that's my cue to go to the lunch line and get some food then," Betty turned, flipping her long, blonde hair, as she headed toward the lunch line.

"Betty, no!" Annette said in a loud whisper. "Don't leave me alone with…" It was too late, Betty was gone, and Joshua was heading in Annette's direction with a full lunch tray in tow.

"Hello, again," Joshua set down his tray which held two slices of pizza and two cartons of chocolate milk.

Annette found her voice. "Eating light, I see."

Joshua chuckled. "Wow! Looks, locker-opening skills and a sense of humor to boot. You're a girl after my own heart."

"Stop, you're making me blush!"

"I noticed that I seem to do that pretty well," Joshua teased.

Annette tried to think of a way to change the subject. "So, did you just move to the area? Where did you live before?"

"Whoa! One question at a time, now!" Joshua smiled. "Yes, we just finished getting everything moved this weekend. I've lived a little bit of everywhere in the past nineteen years. My parents are missionaries, not once a year or during the summer, but all the time. They've been traveling around the world for years, taking me along with them. Not an easy way to grow up, but it was exciting and I got to see a lot of different cultures. I've experienced a lot of things most American teens only read about. Still, my parents decided I should finish up high school in a nice, quiet little town, and they found a great deal on a house out here. Besides, the university I'm planning to go to is only a half hour drive from here, so it will be an easy commute come fall."

"Missionaries? So are they Christian?"

"Yeah, they are. I'd like to think I am, as well. Why do you look so surprised?"

"Well," Annette stammered. "It's just that in my experience, boys that are as, um, open as you, that hasn't really been the case." Annette heard her own words and realized how silly they sounded.

"Ah, you mean that since I'm such a big flirt, you figured I'm some smooth-talking ladies man instead of a boy with a good, Christian background. I see what you think of me now." Joshua pretended to be hurt.

"I didn't mean it that way!" Annette countered.

Joshua chuckled. "I'm just teasing you. Moving around as much as I have, I've found that being outgoing helps me make new friends, which I've had to do often. I have friends around the world and I wouldn't have changed a thing about my life. But I am ready to settle down in one place for a change. And I think I'm really going to like it here."

"And why is that?" Annette asked.

"Because, even though I've been to many places around the world, I've never seen a girl as beautiful as you are."

Chapter Three- The Invitation

For the rest of the week, Joshua sat at Annette and Betty's lunch table. Annette started feeling more and more comfortable talking to Joshua and the blush stopped coming to her cheeks every time he was around. Joshua had all kinds of interesting stories about places he'd traveled to, and he impressed the girls with all the languages he could speak fluently.

The three shared their experiences with church, and told their stories about when God had first came into their lives. "Your church sounds great." Joshua told the two girls one day. "Would you mind if my family came to the service this weekend? We haven't found a church home here yet, of course.'

"We would love to have you and your family at our church," Annette told him. "I look forward to seeing you there."

Most Saturday nights, Betty and her ten-year old sister Sandy came over to spend the night with Annette and Alisa. Sunday morning they all got up and got ready, then Betty and Sandy rode with Annette's family to church.

Betty's parents were divorced, and her mother didn't go to church, despite Betty's efforts to get her to come. She always seemed to have other things to do and would say that maybe she'd come up the following weekend, but she had yet to visit the church at all. She didn't mind her daughters spending the night with Annette's family and going to church with her, however. Betty figured she was probably grateful to have a little break from being a single mom. It was hard on all of them not having a father around.

That Sunday, Annette got out of bed a little earlier than usual. She went over to her vanity table to look at her reflection. She ran a brush through her long, thick auburn waves. *Should I try something different with my hair?* She wondered.

Betty woke up and walked behind Annette, looking at her friend's porcelain skin and green eyes framed with dark lashes. "I know what you're thinking, Annette. You don't need to change a thing about yourself. Not for Joshua, not for anybody. You are beautiful just the way you are."

"I was just thinking that I'm going to meet Joshua's parents this morning. I want to make a good impression. I know I've only known Joshua for a week but I could see myself really liking him."

"I know," Betty responded. "Joshua really likes *you*, I can tell. Of course his parents will like you too. All you have to do is be yourself and I know they will."

Annette gave Betty a big hug. "Thank you, Betty. You always know just what to say."

"Hey, what are best friends for?"

"Don't make me cry, Betty!"

Both girls laughed, and then they broke out of their embrace and started getting ready for church.

*   *   *

Annette's family always arrived at their church a little early so that they could enjoy the fellowship with other members and guests before the service began. Annette went through the normal routine of shaking people's hands, giving hugs to friends, and welcoming visitors. On this particular morning, however, she was also keeping an eye out for Joshua and his parents.

When Joshua walked through the door, Annette's heart felt like it would beat its way right out of her chest. Joshua looked very handsome in his black suit with a shiny, periwinkle-colored dress shirt underneath. The color made his eyes look even more intense than usual.

Joshua's father was tall, just like his son, with broad shoulders and dark hair. The father-son resemblance was striking. Joshua's mother looked very petite next to the two men. She had pale blonde hair and a friendly, welcoming smile. She had a twinkle in her light blue eyes, which were the only thing she seemed to have passed down to her son.

Annette caught her breath and went over to Joshua so that he could introduce her to his parents. "Mom, dad, this is Annette Wilkins, the girl from school that I've told you about."

Annette stepped forward to offer a hand for Joshua's mother to shake but Mrs. Burton had other ideas. She welcomed Annette with a warm hug. "We've heard so much about you, Annette. From what our son says, you're a wonderful young woman. I know he's only known you for a week now but he's a very good judge of character. Thank you so much for inviting our family to your church."

The foursome chatted for a while, and then the rest of the Wilkins family came over to introduce themselves as well. They all talked like old friends until they had to go to the sanctuary to be seated for the service.

Annette was filled with relief. Joshua's parents really seemed to like her. They liked her so much, in fact, that they invited her out to lunch with them after the service was over. Annette felt honored. Her parents insisted that she go with the Burtons, and they would see to it that Betty and Sandy got home. Annette sat next to Joshua during the church service, and managed to concentrate on the pastor's wonderful sermon, even though she was incredibly excited about the lunch with Joshua and his parents.

*   *   *

The conversation never ceased throughout lunch. Joshua's parents asked Annette about her family and her faith, and

Annette had plenty of questions about their mission work. She told them about her nursing school plans and they pointed out all of the mission opportunities that were available for nurses.

Annette hated for the lunch to end, but eventually it had to and the Burton family dropped her off at her house. Joshua insisted on walking Annette to her door. "I had a really good time today, Joshua. I appreciate your parents inviting me along for lunch."

"Annette, they know I'm crazy about you. You're all I've talked about all week. I'm just glad they think you're as special as I do." Joshua reached for Annette's hand and gave it a gentle squeeze before releasing it. He gave Annette one of his famous smiles, and then walked back to his car.

Annette watched Joshua and his parents drive away, then she collapsed onto the porch swing with a sigh. She had known Joshua just a short period of time, but nobody had ever made her feel the way he did. And deep down she had a feeling that he felt the same way about her too.

Alisa pulled back the curtain and peeked through the front window at Annette. *I guess I'll have to go inside,* Annette told herself. She would've rather sat out there the rest of the afternoon daydreaming about Joshua. She knew she couldn't, though. Her family was probably curious about hearing the details of her lunch.

After spending the rest of the afternoon with her family, Annette was anxious for bedtime to come so she could once again be alone with her thoughts. Joshua filled all of them. As she drifted off to sleep, he filled her dreams all night as well.

*   *   *

Annette loved spending lunch with both Betty and Joshua, but she found herself wishing she could have some time with just Joshua. She felt guilty about wishing her best friend wasn't around sometimes, but she liked Joshua so much. Annette was thrilled when Joshua asked her out on a real date on Saturday night.

The rest of the week seemed to drag by as Annette was ready for the weekend to get there. Betty was busy with play rehearsals the whole weekend, so Annette didn't feel too bad about having Saturday plans.

Betty had the lead in the community theatre's adaptation of "Romeo and Juliet." She was a wonderful actress who was in her school's drama class and the International Thespian Society. Betty's dream was to someday be on Broadway, and Annette believed she had the talent and determination to make it.

Annette expressed her artistic side in a different way than Betty. She wasn't one who thrived on being on stage in front of a crowd. She preferred to use her creativity to write. She wrote stories often with a character named Jessica, a young girl who was dealt a rather tough hand of cards.

Jessica's mom was neglectful, even sometimes abusive, but Jessica still was a strong person. She even wrote poetry sometimes with Jessica as the main character. It was fun to put herself into the shoes of someone who had such a different life than hers, even though it made her sad to think of people who were so much less fortunate than she was.

Friday Betty walked Annette home from school. "The guy playing Romeo is soooo cute, Annette. I can't wait for my play practice Saturday. I'll call you to tell you about it and to find out how your date went with you own Romeo!"

Both girls laughed. Betty was not like Annette at all when it came to boys. She had a different crush every week it seemed and was never too crazy about any one boy. The girls hugged each other good bye since they wouldn't see each other again until Sunday at church. "Good luck with your play practice!" Annette told her friend once they were in front of her house.

"And good luck with you-know-who, not that you need it. That boy is just as smitten with you as you are with him," Betty replied.

Annette sighed. "I guess it's no secret I'm crazy about Joshua. I hope I can sleep tonight! I'm so excited about our first 'real' date, you know."

"I know, Annette. But don't worry. It will be great!" Betty flashed Annette a big smile. "You are so lucky, just calm down and have a good time."

"I hope I can! I wish I was more like you, you never get nervous around boys!"

"But I've never found one that I liked as much as you like Joshua either."

"Me neither, Betty. I just hope this feeling lasts a long time."

"Seeing the two of you together, I have no doubt at all that it will, Annette."

Chapter Four- The First Date

That night Annette picked out her clothes carefully. She wanted to look a little dressier than usual but still casual. She picked out a cute jumper that she thought would accomplish this. She *did* have a hard time getting to sleep, but finally managed to drift off and didn't wake until morning.

When getting ready for her date, Annette even put on a little lip gloss, which she rarely wore. Everyone else saw Annette as a natural beauty, although she didn't think she was anything special. Others saw something in her that she rarely saw in herself. She spent a few extra minutes getting her hair just right.

Annette only had toast for breakfast, telling her mom she didn't want to spoil her appetite for lunch, but her mother gave her a knowing look. She knew nerves were more to blame than worrying about a spoiled appetite.

"So, what do you and Joshua have planned for today? I assume you're going to lunch, since you don't want to 'spoil your appetite.' Do you know where?" Mrs. Wilkins asked her daughter.

"Actually, I'm not sure, mom. He's picking me up at noon and he told me not to have lunch beforehand, but I'm not sure exactly where we're going. I assume we are going out to eat since he told me not to eat."

"Oh, a surprise. How romantic," Annette's mom said, her eyes dreamy. She was remembering her first dates with her husband. The romance and mystery were so exciting. Although she was happy with their relationship at this point of their lives, it was fun to look back to when everything was so fresh and new.

"What's romantic, sweetheart?" Annette's father asked as he entered the room and gave his wife a kiss.

"Joshua is picking me up at 12 for our first date and it's a surprise where we're going." Annette told her dad.

"I was just remembering when you used to do things like that for me," Mrs. Wilkins teased her husband.

"I see. Well, tomorrow after church I'm taking *you* on a surprise date. Will you watch your sister for us, please, Annette?"

"Sure, dad," Annette was glad her parents were still so much in love after all these years. She could see in their eyes how much they loved each other. So many of her schoolmates had gone through the divorce of their parents, including Betty. It gave her hope to see her parents so happy after almost twenty years of marriage. They seemed to grow more deeply in love with each passing year.

"That reminds me, our anniversary is coming up in June, right after Annette's graduation. Twenty years is a pretty big one," Annette's mom pointed out.

"Now that you mention it, twenty is a pretty big number. I might have to pull together something special this year," Mr. Wilkins hugged his wife and gave Annette a wink where his wife could not see it. Annette already knew about his plans to take her mother on a romantic second honeymoon the week of their anniversary. Since Annette would be out of school she was going to baby sit and take care of the house. They were going to the same resort they went to on their real honeymoon. He had already made the arrangements and swore Annette to secrecy so he could surprise his wife.

Annette tried to keep herself busy with chores until noon so she would be too occupied to worry. The door bell rang at 11:45. "He's early!" Annette exclaimed before ducking into the bathroom to quickly freshen up.

Mr. Wilkins opened the door and let Joshua into the living room where the two sat to chat for a few minutes. Annette grabbed her purse and took one final glance in the mirror. She took a deep breath and slowly let it out to calm her nerves before stepping into the living room.

"Hi, Annette. You look great," Joshua greeted her.

"Thank you," Annette tried to keep from blushing, even though Joshua was used to it by now and thought it was cute.

"Well, I'll let you kids get on your way," Annette's dad shook Joshua's hand and pulled him a bit closer to say, "Take care of my daughter."

"I will, sir,' Joshua said, looking Mr. Wilkins square in the eye.

"I'm sure you will. I can already tell that you're a fine young man, Joshua."

Joshua grinned, and then escorted Annette out to his car. He opened the passenger side door for her, and then said, "I think your dad likes me."

"Thank goodness," Annette said. She was always nervous about her father meeting a date. He was very protective of his firstborn daughter, and it was very important to her that her father approve. She was glad that part was over, and she was ready to change the subject. "So, where are we going?"

"I told you, that's a surprise. You'll find out when we get there."

They drove a while, chatting about school and their mutual friends. The pair eventually pulled up at Shadyside Park. Joshua got out of the car and led Annette to an open area with a big blanket spread out. There was a large picnic basket filled with sandwiches and fresh fruit, thermoses of soup, and water bottles filled with fresh-squeezed lemonade.

"Oh, Joshua! You must have been getting this ready all morning!"

"Well, I get up early anyway. And it was all worth it, just to bring that beautiful smile to your face. Have a seat." He patted a place on the blanket next to him.

Joshua began pulling things out of the picnic basket. "Hey! How did this get in there?" he handed Annette a pink carnation.

"How did you know that was my favorite flower?"

"You must have mentioned it, or maybe someone else you know did. Who keeps track of such things?" Annette knew he must have asked someone to make sure every detail was perfect.

"Joshua, it's beautiful. Thank you!"

"Not as beautiful as you are." He touched Annette on the nose, then leaned over and softly kissed Annette's slightly parted, waiting lips. Their first kiss was small, but very sweet.

They spent the rest of the afternoon in the park--eating their lunches, walking hand-in-hand around the nature trails and throwing a Frisbee with some children who came to the park to play. Annette loved that Joshua seemed to love children as much as she did. She knew in her heart that no matter how things turned out, Annette would remember this date forever.

Chapter Five- A Change Of Plans

From that day forward, Annette and Joshua were inseparable. They went out every weekend, sometimes just the two of them, but sometimes they double dated with Betty and her most recent "Romeo," Alex. By the time graduation rolled around in June, they both knew that they were in love.

Immediately after graduation, Annette and her family went on vacation to the beach. She knew that she would miss Joshua terribly, but Annette was also looking forward to one last vacation with her family. Since she would be going off to college and beginning to work, the days of family vacations with all four of them were coming to an end.

Annette enjoyed her vacation very much. She never got to spend enough time with Alisa and during the vacation the sisters had plenty of time together. Annette took her baby sister out for smoothies at a great little shop right off the beach, they went swimming together, went sight-seeing, and they bought tacky souvenirs to bring back to their friends.

One day towards the end of the week-long vacation, Annette and Alisa went walking barefoot along the beach. They looked for unusual seashells to take home and they dipped their feet in the cold ocean water.

Alisa was kicking water at her big sister when a young blonde guy approached to them. He was tanned and wearing swim trunks. "Hi, my name is Patrick," the young man told Annette, holding out his hand for her to shake.

"So, would the two of you like to join our beach volleyball game?" Patrick asked.

"No, I wouldn't care to," Annette quickly told him. "I would certainly be holding back whichever team I played for. I'm far too uncoordinated for organized sports. I have a habit of tripping over my own feet. I swear I tripped over a line someone had drawn on the floor just the other day."

Patrick laughed heartily. Alisa looked at her sister with a sly smile. She knew that Patrick was trying to flirt, as the joke was not nearly *that* funny.

"Okay, then. I won't force you to play. How about going out to dinner with me tonight instead?" Patrick flashed a brilliant white smile at Annette.

"I'm sorry, Patrick, but I have a boyfriend back at home who wouldn't like that very much," Annette said politely.

"Well, I won't tell him if you won't," Patrick insisted. "That's what vacations are for," he winked.

"Not for me, mine is for spending time with my family. Come on sis, let's get back to our parents," Annette grabbed Alisa's hand and the two of them walked away with a bewildered Patrick left standing in the sand.

"Okay, your loss then," Patrick called out.

"No, I don't think so," Annette shouted back.

"Can you believe that guy?" Alisa asked her big sister with wide eyes.

"That's how some guys are. That makes me feel even more blessed to have Joshua. And now I miss him more than ever," Annette suddenly felt very sad and couldn't wait to get back to the beach house and call her boyfriend.

* * *

Annette counted down the miles on the way home from her family vacation. It wasn't just because she hated long car trips. Joshua was coming over as soon as they got back. The week had felt so much longer than seven days without seeing him. She hadn't even been able to call him that often.

When they pulled up to the house, Annette was surprised to see Joshua sitting on the front porch waiting for their return. She ran towards him and he met her halfway, sweeping her up into his arms.

"Joshua! What are you doing here? How did you know when I'd be home?" Annette asked.

"Well, you called and let me know when you were leaving so I tried to figure out about when you'd get home. I was about a half hour off," he explained.

"It's so hot out here! And you waited out on the porch for me for thirty minutes?" Annette was touched.

"Of course I did. I missed you so much that I couldn't wait another minute to see you. Not even the time it took for me to drive over after you got home and called me," Joshua gently pushed Annette's hair back from her face and kissed the tip of her nose.

"You know what? I think I love you," Annette teased.

"Well, I know I love you. And I have proof," Joshua broke their embrace long enough to go to his car and grab a composition book from the passenger seat.

"I wrote this for you. At first I was going to just write you letters but then I figured I'd put them in a notebook so you could keep it and always remember how much I hated being away from you. I wrote you a letter each time I thought about you," Joshua looked down, blushing. It was hard for a guy to admit such feelings.

Annette flipped through the book. As she kept flipping, hot tears splattered down both cheeks. The entire notebook was full, each page covered with words of affection, front and back.

* * *

Luckily, Annette's nursing school and the University Joshua planned to attend were close enough that the couple could meet occasionally during the week, in addition to their dates on weekends. Not seeing each other very often made the time that they *did* get to spend together even more precious, and they didn't waste a minute of the time they had together.

Annette's second love was nursing school. She was interested in learning all the procedures and scientific aspects of the profession, as science had always been a favorite subject of hers. Even more than that, she loved interacting with her patients during her clinical assignments.

Annette loved nursing even more than she thought she would. Even though she had a soft spot in her heart for children and babies, she also loved working with the elderly. Most of the little old ladies she cared for were sweet, and many reminded her of her dear Nana.

The first time a patient told her that she was going to make a great nurse, Annette's heart melted. She loved helping people, and although the job was far from easy at times, she loved the feeling she got from knowing she was helping people, even in some small way.

During busy shifts, when she felt like it was getting to be too much, there was always something to let her know she was making a difference. A patient would say "You're so nice," or "Thank you for helping me—I don't know what I would do without such great nurses," then Annette would get a second wind and be ready for the rest of her shift.

Joshua was studying Engineering at the University. While he was keeping up his grades, Annette noticed that his heart just didn't seem to be in what he was doing. One weekend Joshua seemed to be particularly down and Annette asked him what was wrong. He finally opened up to her about what had been bothering him.

"Annette, I've been doing a lot of thinking. Engineering is a great profession, and I would have a lot of opportunities and it would pay well, but I'm just not sure I would be happy doing it for the rest of my life. I don't love it the way you love your nursing. I was interested in my classes at first, since everything was new and exciting, but now it feels so—I don't know—empty, I guess that's the best way I can describe what I'm feeling."

"Have you prayed about it, Joshua? Asked God to lead you in the path he has planned for your life?

"Probably not as much as I should," Joshua admitted, looking   down   at   the   ground.
        "Why don't you try that, Joshua? It always helps me."

Joshua grinned. "You always know just what to say, Annette. Your patients are going to be so lucky to have you for a nurse." Annette blushed at the compliment, but forgot about her embarrassment as Joshua pulled her close to him for a sweet thank you kiss.

Joshua put a lot of thought into what Annette had said. The next weekend, his demeanor was completely different. "I did what you suggested, Annette. I gave it to God. I asked Him to lead to what he wanted me to do. Last night I was having the most beautiful dream. I woke up in the middle of the night, remembering the dream so vividly, and I had something in my heart. I just knew it was God leading me to what I was meant to do."

Annette held her breath waiting for Joshua to go on. "What is it, Joshua?"

"I'm going to go into ministry. I want to be a pastor. In my dream I had this small cozy little church in a small area like your hometown. Not a big fancy church with stained-glass windows and big spending accounts, but a simple small-town church, one that can grow, but will always feel like home. Okay, I'm rambling now. What are you thinking Annette?"

"I think it's a great idea," Annette said after releasing her breath and giving Joshua a big hug. "It's wonderful. But are there any seminary schools around here? I don't know of any."

"That's the only problem I see, Annette. The closest one is hours away. I don't mind that, except that I wouldn't get to see you as often. Do you think we could make it?"

"Joshua, I love you. I would miss you terribly, of course, even more than I do now, but I know we could make it. I want you to be happy more than anything else, you know that."

"Of course I do, Annette. We could still see each other on the weekends. It wouldn't be all that much worse than it is now, really." Joshua said, but sounded like he was trying to convince himself as much as he was Annette.

"I suppose not. Then again, my classes are starting to get a lot harder. I'm starting to have a lot of homework on the weekends." Annette started to sound worried.

"Annette, we have to make this work. We love each other way too much not to. You know as well as I do that I can't ignore this calling from God. I hope you wouldn't ask me to give up this dream. I would never ask you to give up nursing, you know that."

"Yes, of course I do," Annette answered. "And I would never ask you not to go into ministry. I can tell you're so much happier just thinking about and talking about it."

"I am, Annette. Even though I'm worried and sad about the time I'll be away from you, I already feel like my life has more meaning now. Can I count on you to support me through this, even if times get hard for us?"

"Do you even have to ask?" Annette grinned. "Of course I will be there for you always, Joshua, no matter what you choose."

Joshua pulled Annette into a tight embrace. A single tear gleamed out of the corner of his eye. He said a silent prayer that what Annette had just said would always be true.

CHAPTER SIX-THE CHRISTMAS SURPRISE

The next months were indeed very hard on the couple. Joshua couldn't afford the long commute every weekend to come back and see Annette and his family. The frequent long distance phone calls became expensive as well. He ended up taking a part-time job near his school, working every other weekend, and coming back home to visit on alternating weekends.

Annette and Joshua never seemed to be able to spend enough time together, or talk often enough, but their love stayed strong. They wrote long love letters between calls and visits, and both of them read them over and over when they felt lonely. Despite the distance, their love grew stronger, and when Joshua came back home for Christmas break, he had a surprise for Annette.

Joshua knelt in front of Annette on Christmas day in front of both of their families and said, "Annette, I love you more than life itself. I would be most honored if you'd agree to be my wife." Alissa squealed with surprise and delight, but Annette's parents just gazed at one another with a smile and reached out to squeeze each other's hands. They had known this was coming as Joshua had asked for their blessing beforehand and they had enthusiastically granted it.

Annette was so emotional, she could barely speak, but managed to squeak out a "yes" and she hugged Joshua tightly and cried while their families cheered. Joshua had asked everyone if they could all celebrate Christmas together since he and Annette wanted to spend time with each other as well as the rest of their families, but everyone had suspicions that this moment was upon them. Nobody wanted to miss this occasion, or tear the couple apart that was so deeply in love.

Later that afternoon, Annette and Joshua finally got a few minutes alone. They cuddled together on the front porch swing and watched tiny snowflakes fall. They were only having flurries and it wasn't really sticking, but it was beautiful and added a special touch to the day that had already been filled with so much celebration.

"Joshua, I am so happy," Annette said as she gazed at the simple, small heart-shaped diamond on her finger. "I want nothing more than to be your wife."

"I only wish I could have afforded a better ring for you, one that matched how much I love you. But they don't make diamonds that big, and I had to save from every one of my paychecks just to be able to buy you that little one. Maybe later I can go back and get you a bigger one."

"Don't you dare, Joshua Burton! This one is perfect! Besides, it's the one you put on my finger when you asked me to marry you and that made it more special than any other ring in the world. I absolutely love it!"

"I absolutely love *you*, the future Mrs. Burton."

"I could get used to being called that," Annette teased, and then she sank into Joshua's arms, feeling like the luckiest girl who ever lived. She didn't even feel the cold when Joshua was holding her.

CHAPTER SEVEN-AN UNEXPECTED ARRIVAL

After winter break ended, it was back to school for Joshua and Annette. Annette kept working as a nursing assistant for the home health care agency on the same weekends that Joshua worked and put aside money for her and Joshua's life together.

Annette had decided to go through a program that allowed her to take the state board exam to become an LPN and work as a licensed nurse while she was still taking classes to get to her ultimate goal of becoming a Registered Nurse.

She was ecstatic when she passed the LPN state boards. She was a nurse now.

Joshua tried to convince Annette to marry him that summer. He reasoned that she could move near him, work part time as a nurse and change schools to one near his seminary. Annette, however, was adamant that they do things the "right way." She wanted to finish school and save up for a nice wedding that they would never be able to afford right then.

With both of them working and studying so much, the next year and a half rushed by in a blur as it was and Annette had finally reached her goal. Everyone was beaming with pride as they watched her graduate and receive her nurse's hat and pin.

Annette took a full-time job in the hospital near her home where she had volunteered so many years before. She started out as a "float nurse," which meant that she got assigned to various departments of the hospital, depending on where the greatest need was that day.

Some nurses didn't like floating, because they never knew where they would be working, and some liked a more structured routine, but Annette loved it. It kept the job from getting mundane, although it seldom was anyway, and it gave her the chance to meet lots of new people. She also got to use lots of different nursing skills. Annette especially loved working in pediatrics and Labor and Delivery since she loved babies and children.

Annette's time with Joshua was more limited than ever, so it was good that she was keeping busy with work. She made friends with a girl named Nancy at work who was engaged to a man in the military, because they understood what each other were going through.

Ever since Betty had been accepted to a performing arts school in New York and moved away, she never seemed to have enough time to talk to Annette. Annette continued to write to Betty when she got a chance. She often called Betty but usually got her voicemail and rarely got a call back. When Betty did call she complained that she was either too busy to call or said she didn't have money for the long distance bill and didn't want to call collect.

Annette became concerned about her oldest and dearest friend. Betty was a good person, but she seemed to follow the crowd a bit too much once she got to college. The last time she had called her friend, Betty had sounded like she'd been drinking and had lots of classmates over that were laughing and having a good time in the background. Of course Betty had quickly hung up the phone, saying she had guests to entertain.

One evening after work, Annette was resting in her room, propping up her aching feet. The phone rang, and her mother came in with the cordless handset. "It's for you, Annette. It's Betty. She sounds upset. Annette was surprised to hear that since she hadn't spoken to her friend in weeks. At the sound of Annette's voice, Betty broke out into uncontrollable sobs.

"Betty, what's wrong? Are you okay? Are you hurt?"

Betty struggled to catch her breath and control her voice. "No, Annette. I'm not okay. I've messed up my whole life, and I have nobody to blame but myself."

"Just take a deep breath and try to relax enough to tell me what happened, Betty. I'm sure it's not as bad as you're thinking." Betty always had a dramatic flair, so there was no way to tell if she'd been in a terrible car accident, or if her boyfriend of the week had broken up with her.

"Okay," Betty took in a deep breath. "I'm pregnant."

Annette nearly dropped the phone. She wasn't expecting that kind of news. "Oh, my! What are you going to do, Betty? Are you going to get married?"

"No, that's what makes the whole situation even worse. When Alex found out I was pregnant, he left! He was staying here with me and helping me pay my bills. Both of my parents have been mad at me and stopped sending me money ever since they found out Alex was living with me," Betty blew her nose and continued.

"My job waiting tables only pays about half of the rent and expenses. I was counting on Alex for the other half. I thought he loved me, Annette. I never expected he would freak out when he found out I was pregnant. It's not like I got this way by myself! Oh, Annette. Now I don't know what to do," Betty took a deep breath and let out a big sigh.

"First of all, Betty, call your parents and talk to them. Let them know that you've made some mistakes but you're sorry. Hopefully one of them will let you live with them. You can't stay up there and go to college and take care of a baby by yourself," Annette said.

"I know, I can't even take care of myself right now. But I already called my parents and talked to them, Annette. I begged both of them to let me come back," Betty was on the verge of tears.

"What did they say, sweetie?" Annette knew from Betty's tone that it was not good news.

"They said I couldn't move back in with either of them. They said I need to take responsibility for my own actions. They said I'm not a child any more and it's time I started acting like an adult and taking care of myself. They couldn't agree on anything else, that's why they got a divorce, but they agreed on that.

"But, Betty, you're their daughter! They wouldn't put you out on the streets, would they?"

"My parents aren't like yours, Annette. They aren't very forgiving. I just don't know where to turn."

"Well, you know I will always be your friend, no matter what mistakes you've made in your life. I hope you never forget that."

"I don't know what I'd do without you," Betty said, sniffling.

After hanging up the phone, Annette had a long talk with her parents and let them know everything that was going on with Betty. The three decided that if Betty needed to stay with them for a while, she could. Betty had been like a daughter to them when the girls were in school, and they felt it was their duty as Christians to help out a young girl in need.

A couple of weeks later, Annette met Betty at the bus station to bring her back to the Wilkins' home. Annette was surprised to see how round Betty's abdomen was already. She couldn't help asking, "Betty, how far along are you?"

"I don't know. Three months, four maybe. Not exactly sure," Betty shrugged.

Annette pursed her lips and raised one of her eyebrows. "You mean you haven't been to see a doctor at all—through your whole pregnancy?"

"No, I haven't," Betty sighed. "I didn't have any money or any insurance. What was I supposed to do? I wasn't even sure I was pregnant at first. Maybe I was just too scared to admit it to myself. I've never been good at keeping track of when my period is due. I guess I started showing really early because I'm a little on the small side, and I couldn't deny it any longer."

Annette reasoned that what Betty said could be true. Betty was barely over five feet tall and weighed about a hundred pounds on a good day, so her baby didn't have too much to hide behind. Annette also knew that denial could be a powerful thing for someone who really didn't want to believe she was pregnant. She had seen patients come in about to deliver that were denying it was possible for them to be pregnant.

"Well, we are going to get you and that baby in to see a doctor as soon as possible now."

Annette kept her promise. She talked to an obstetrician she worked with at the hospital who fit Betty into her schedule that week. The doctor wanted to do an ultrasound. Since Betty had no money or insurance, the doctor did it without charging as a favor to Annette.

The doctor took measurements and said "It looks like your baby is at about five month's gestation. Everything looks good. I don't see any abnormalities in development. I can even see the sex if you want to know."

"What is it?" Betty asked.

"Looks like a boy, although ultrasound is not always right, I'm pretty sure this time," the doctor turned the ultrasound screen towards Betty and Annette.

"Wow, look at that, Betty. See the little nose and chin? The little fingers and toes," Annette looked at the screen in awe. She had always been fascinated by the development of a baby in a mother's womb and couldn't wait for the day she would have a baby with Joshua.

"I can't tell what's what on these things. It's like trying to see something in an ink blot," Betty sighed.

The doctor gave Betty information on eating right during her pregnancy and gave her lots of samples for prenatal vitamins. Annette took Betty home, saying a silent prayer of thanks that the baby appeared to be healthy despite having no prenatal care for the past five months. She had hoped that Betty would become more excited about the baby after seeing the ultrasound though. Some women didn't seem to connect with their babies until the birth. She hoped that would be true for Betty.

Betty stayed with the Wilkins family for the remainder of her pregnancy. The months flew by with all of the planning for the arrival of the new baby, as well as the preparation for Annette and Joshua's upcoming wedding.

CHAPTER EIGHT-
PREPARA-
TIONS

Annette was still worried about Betty, but she tried to concentrate as much of her energy as she could on her upcoming wedding. After hearing that the baby and Betty were healthy, she allowed herself to get caught up in details of her fast-approaching nuptials. She had dreamed of what her wedding would be like since she was a little girl, and she wanted it to be as perfect as it was in her imagination when she had a head full of auburn ringlets.

Betty was excited about the wedding, but Annette couldn't help noticing a bit of envy in her friend's eyes when she tried on an ivory, strapless gown. Betty seemed so sad. "You know what, Betty? I can come back here and try on dresses later with Alissa and my mom to help me. Why don't I take you out to lunch at your favorite restaurant, my treat? Is it still Bellini's?"

"Yes…Okay," Betty seemed a bit excited at the unexpected offer. "I haven't been there in ages. The food in New York is good, but just not the same as what I grew up with. My parents used to take me to Bellini's back when I was a kid, before the divorce, and I have so many good memories there."

"Well, the two of us can go there and make new memories. Just let me take off these layers of taffeta," both girls laughed as Annette acting as if she was drowning in the poofy dress.

At lunch the two talked and laughed, and it felt like the good old days again. They brought up acquaintances from back in high school and tried to guess what some of them were doing now.

"Hey, remember Marty Howser? He was planning to be the next Bill Gates. Have you seen him around?" Betty asked Annette.

"Oh, yes. I saw him just the other day. He is working at the computer repair shop downtown. He married Erma Wells and they had twin daughters!"

"Yeah, president of Microsoft or repairing used computers, same difference," Betty shrugged and sipped her smoothie.

Annette laughed and said, "Well, they seem happy and that's all that matters. This was the Betty that she missed, the one she hadn't seen in such a long time. "I'm really having a great time, Betty. We need to do this more often."

"Betty? Annette? Oh how *are* you girls?" The two friends looked up to see Pryscilla Mills, one of the most popular girls from their high school. Her long silky blonde hair was full of highlights and her dark tan really emphasized her sparkling blue eyes.

"We're fine. Just enjoying a break from planning Annette's wedding," Betty said. Annette noticed that Betty crossed her arms over her large belly and leaned forward a bit, as if she were trying to hide her protruding abdomen beneath the edge of the table.

"Yes, I heard about Annette's ceremony. Sounds rather, how should I say this? Quaint." She gave the two girls a sarcastic smile. "Tim Rawlings and I are getting married next summer, we're flying all of our family and close friends to Jamaica for our wedding. We're taking along our own caterers though, of course," It was hard not to notice the huge two and a half carat ring that Pryscilla flashed within view every chance she got.

"Sounds lovely, Pryscilla. I just want a nice, simple affair. I don't need anything that fancy. Though I'm sure yours will be very nice as well," Annette turned back to Betty. "Would you like to order desert?" She was trying to give Pryscilla a subtle hint that the girls weren't interested in her bragging.

"I don't think Betty needs any dessert. She looks like she's gained quite a bit of weight there…hey wait a minute. Perhaps it wasn't too much desert, but too much of another indulgence," Pryscilla laughed at her own joke. "I guess congratulations are in order Betty. I must have missed word of *your* wedding."

"Thanks, Pryscilla. Betty appreciates your good wishes, but we need to get back to our food and our planning. I'm sure you have your own lunch to get to," Annette said. She looked over at Betty who couldn't decide whether to be angry or hurt at Pryscilla's words. She knew the girl had just said those things to be mean.

"Oh, Betty, don't pay her any mind," Annette put her hand on her friend's shoulder. "She's just a hateful person who likes to rub it in people's faces that she has what they don't. We'll pray for her, okay?"

"It's not just her, Annette. I see how other people look at me. This is not what I had planned for my life," with that Betty dissolved into tears. "I haven't done any of the things I wanted to accomplish in my life. I'm not married, and I'm pregnant with a baby I don't even know how I'm going to care for, that I don't even want most of the time!"

"Now, Betty. I don't want to hear you say such things! You are going to be a good mom. You are going to take one look at that baby and fall in love with him. A baby is not a mistake, even when it's not planned, it's a gift from God. And one day you will find a nice, decent man who will love both you and your baby. You'll accomplish your goals. You just have to believe in yourself."

A tear sprang to Betty's eye. "Annette, I wish I had your faith. I always wanted to be more like you. I just can't think the way that you do. Things don't work out for me the way that they do for you. You never would have been unfortunate enough to get pregnant before you were married."

"Betty, luck had nothing to do with that. I made a vow to myself, to God, and to my future husband to save myself for marriage. I've kept that vow, so I've never had to worry about becoming pregnant out of wedlock. I know that may sound harsh or condescending to you, but it's not luck that has determined my fate, but the choices I have made for myself."

Annette could see a flicker of jealousy in Betty's eye. "I guess I just can't be perfect like you, Annette."

"Now, Betty, I'm not perfect. I'm far from it. And don't believe for a second that it's been easy for me and Joshua to wait all this time. We love each other very much, and waiting is far from an easy thing to do. But we know it will be worth it and we will be glad we waited. I'm so glad I waited for him.

Please don't think I'm trying to make you feel bad about your choices that you've made, but trying to let you know that everything in life has consequences. The decisions you make today can affect your life tomorrow, even if they seem like small decisions.

We all make mistakes, but all you can do after you've made one is pick yourself back up and try to get back on the right path. You're the one who has to help yourself. Nobody else will do it for you."

Betty seemed to take Annette's little talk to heart and tried to look on the bright side a little more in the next weeks. She even started getting more excited about the little details of the wedding, helping Annette pick out the flowers and invitations and decorations.

The night before the wedding, Annette and Betty had their very last slumber party together in Annette's room. After the honeymoon, Annette was of course moving in with Joshua, and Betty was going to live with the couple until she got on her feet. Their apartment was small, and she would have to sleep on the fold-out sofa, but Betty felt more comfortable staying with Annette, even though Annette's parents offered for her to continue living there.

"Annette?" Betty whispered.

"Hmmm?" Annette was about to drift off to sleep.

"Are you nervous about tomorrow?"

"I wouldn't say nervous…well, perhaps a bit. I'm more excited than anything else. I've waited for this day for as long as I can remember. I don't know if I'll sleep at all tonight."

"Annette," Betty started slowly. "I hope you realize how incredibly lucky you are. You have the greatest guy in the world, who's going to be a minister soon. You have the career you've always wanted. You have everything you've ever dreamed of.

I had such big plans for my life. I planned to do some acting, maybe a little modeling. I dreamed of seeing my name up in lights on Broadway. I even got a couple of little modeling jobs before I got pregnant. Nothing major, just car show modeling and such, but it made me feel special, like I was somebody. Now after having a baby, I won't have the same opportunities. I'll have to get a job just to make ends meet. I'll end up settling for a mundane life when I wanted so much more."

"Betty, it's not too late for you to live your dreams. But you have to ask yourself if fortune and fame are what you really want for yourself and for your child? Of course you know you are beautiful, I've always thought you were. Everyone thinks so. But do you really want one of your main goals in life to be modeling, where you are judged on the way that you look without people ever getting to know who you are inside?

I know some people are happy with that profession, but I know you can do a lot with your life Betty. You are very talented. You're very artistic and crafty. You paint beautiful pictures. There are many things you can do. I know that whatever you choose, things will work out for the best."

Betty wiped away her tears. "I sure hope so, Annette. And I know you will always be there to help me, Annette. I don't know what I would have done without you. You're the only one in my life that I can count on."

"I will always be here for you, Betty. That's what best friends are for." Annette went over to gently embrace her friend, and they laughed because Betty's big belly made this a difficult task.

"We'd better get some sleep sometime tonight," Betty said. "Especially you. You have a big day tomorrow and need to look your best," she added.

"And you, too. You have a baby in your belly to take care of, and he needs his rest as well."

Annette finally went to sleep after much tossing and turning. This time instead of dreaming of being saved by a handsome prince, she was dreaming of walking down the aisle with him, in her fairy tale wedding.

CHAPTER NINE- THE WEDDING

"**M**om says it's time to get up, sleepyheads!" Alisa said in a sing-song voice as she opened the mini-blinds and let the sunshine stream through the windows.

"Here comes the bride, all dressed in white," Alisa started singing.

Annette rubbed her eyes. "Okay, okay. The bride is officially awake," she let out a big yawn.

"I can't believe my sister is getting married and moving away," Alisa said. She pouted and crossed her arms across her chest. She couldn't pretend to be upset very long, though. Her smile broke out and she hugged her big sister. "Seriously, I'm so excited for you, Annette, but I'm going to miss you not being here with me all the time."

"Alisa, you know you can come over any time you'd like. We can pop popcorn and watch movies and it will be just like old times. That will even give mom and dad a night alone every now and then."

"That sounds good to me," Mrs. Wilkins laughed from the doorway. "But for now, we all have a wedding to get ready for, so let's get moving!"

The four of them all had appointments to have their hair done that morning. Alisa's long auburn hair was curled into ringlets that hung down her back, and she was going to wear a floral wreath on the crown of her head. At eleven, she was a little on the old side for a flower girl, but she insisted on taking on that role since she had never been one before and she felt like she was too young to be a bridesmaid.

Of course Betty was Annette's maid of honor, and her cousin Angie and her best friend from work, Nancy, were honored to be bridesmaids. All three ladies had their hair pulled back into elegant chignons with little sprigs of baby's breath woven throughout.

Finally, Annette's hair was swept into an updo with a few ringlets framing her face. The hairdresser attached a rhinestone tiara to Annette's hair. It held her long veil in place.

Annette had planned to do her own makeup, but her mom had surprised her with an early wedding gift as a special treat. She paid for Annette to have her makeup done professionally. She had never felt so pampered, and she enjoyed every minute of it.

Alisa captured every special moment with her camera. She had recently decided she wanted to become a photographer when she grew up and she felt it was her duty to take pictures of everyone getting ready for the wedding.

When the hairdresser and makeup artist were done with Annette, everyone stared in amazement. She had always been a pretty girl, but she had been transformed into a stunning beauty right before their eyes.

When Annette saw her reflection, she almost cried at the sight of herself looking so fancy and grown-up.

"Don't cry, you'll smear your mascara, dear," her mom warned, even though she was fighting back tears of her own. "You are the most beautiful bride I've ever seen, and you're not even wearing your dress yet. I know once you're in that, I'll be doing enough crying for both of us."

That broke the tension and everyone started to laugh. "Now, let's get to the church so we can get dressed," Annette announced. "We all look so great that one of us has got to get married."

* * *

"Oh, Annette, I look like a beached whale in this dress," Betty complained.

"You look adorable, Betty, don't be silly," Annette assured her. She meant it, too. The lavender lace did nothing to hide the eight month pregnancy, but Betty was all belly, and did look very cute.

Everyone that saw Betty kept saying she would lose all of her pregnancy weight right after the birth, and Annette believed it. She was secretly wishing to look as great as Betty one day, when she and Joshua were having a baby of their own, even though she'd never been quite as petite as her friend.

"All of you look great," Annette told her bridesmaids after they had all slipped into their lace gowns. "Now I need help getting into *my* dress.

Annette did indeed need help. Her dress had a fitted bodice with little seed pearls and tiny sequins, but below the waist it poofed out into an explosion of taffeta.

She had fallen in love with this dress the first time she laid eyes on it. It fit perfectly and she felt like a princess in it. She looked at many other dresses to be sure, but her mind always went back to that one. Annette felt it was the dress she was born to get married in.

The combination of the beautiful dress with the perfect hair, makeup, and veil did prove to be too much for Annette's mom. She could no longer hold back the tears as she said, "I can't believe my little girl is all grown up and getting married. I've never been so proud, happy, and sad all at the same time in my life."

"Mom, you know that I'll always be your little girl. You're not getting rid of me that easily. Even when I have kids of my own, I'll still be your baby."

"Annette, please don't talk about having your own kids, I can only handle one thing at a time!" They all laughed and blotted away any tears that threatened to run down their faces.

"Well," Annette took a deep breath to calm her nerves. "I guess it's show time."

Mrs. Wilkins took her seat in the front pew while the rest of the girls got situated into position for their journey down the aisle.

Annette closed her eyes for a second and inhaled deeply when she heard the beginning of the song she had chosen for her walk down the aisle. She walked through the entranceway and took her father's arm. She could feel him trembling a bit, just as she was.

Annette thought that although it was such a short walk to the end of the aisle, it had been such a long journey in her life. She met Joshua's eyes from several steps away. He looked more handsome than ever in his white tuxedo. His eyes were fixed on her, his face giving away how beautiful he thought she was at that moment. The couple knew that they had never been more in love than they were at this very moment.

Both of them fought back tears as they recited their vows and shared their first kiss as man and wife. The moment they had both waited so long for was finally here and they both tried to commit every second of it to memory.

The wedding reception went by in a blur of cake, punch, and pictures. Annette and Joshua were leaving that night for their honey-moon after the end of the reception. They loved celebrating with their family and friends, but could barely wait to start their lives together as man and wife.

CHAPTER TEN- THE BIRTH

Joshua and Annette had a wonderful time on their honeymoon. The week flew by for the happy couple as they spent time swimming, sight-seeing, and just enjoying each other's company. As much fun as it was being on vacation, the best part of all for Annette was lying in Joshua's arms at night while she fell asleep. She had never felt so happy, safe, and in love.

The seven days were not enough for the twosome, but both of them needed to get back to work. Joshua was going to start a new job teaching classes at a private Christian school in the fall, but found a summer job to earn some money in the meantime.

Annette was also eager to get back to Betty, who was due in just a few weeks. She was planning to take a few weeks off of work when the baby came to help out also, so she couldn't take any more time off after the wedding.

The couple got adjusted quickly to married life, even though Betty complained about feeling like a fifth wheel. Annette enjoyed decorating the apartment when she had a rare free moment. She picked a ladybug theme for the bathroom and a daisy theme for the bedroom. Joshua shook his head and teased her about trying to make the house look girly, but he really didn't mind. Nothing was as important to him as making his new bride happy.

Annette was so busy throughout the last weeks of Betty's pregnancy that time flew for her. For Betty, it was quite another story. Time seemed to drag on, each day an eternity as she watched her body grow to sizes she had never dreamed of.

One afternoon Annette arrived home from work to find Betty stretched out on the sofa watching television. She had her shirt pulled up to reveal her large round belly. "Wow, it's gotten really big," Annette observed.

Betty shot her a glance that said *careful*. "Watch, Annette." Annette eyed her friend's belly, the skin taut and shiny as it stretched over her unborn baby. Suddenly Annette saw Betty's belly jump over towards one side.

Annette laughed. "Wow, he's quite the little kicker there, isn't he? Perhaps he will be a great soccer star one day? What does that feel like, a baby kicking inside of you?"

Betty took her friend's hand and gently placed it in the place where her unborn child had just kicked. At first the baby seemed to have settled down. "That figures. Babies never kick when you want them to," Annette smiled.

As if to prove her wrong, the baby gave her a big thump right against her hand. Both girls laughed. "Wow, that must feel really neat, a new life growing inside, getting bigger, totally dependent on you," Annette gave her friend a wistful smile.

"Yeah, you'd think so, until the baby kicks your ribs or gives you heartburn!" Betty quipped.

Each day that passed, Betty joked less and complained more about the pregnancy. She waddled when she walked, and every time she thought her belly couldn't get any bigger, it did. She felt like she would be the only person in the world to ever be pregnant forever.

She complained about her back aching constantly and frequently said that she would be much happier once this baby decided to come out. Annette gently reminded her that taking care of a baby was not going to be any easier than being pregnant.

Several people from the church donated baby items for Betty, since they knew she was in a bad situation. Betty planned to go back to work when the baby was six weeks old and save up enough money to get her own apartment.

Mrs. Wilkins offered to baby sit for Betty so she wouldn't have to pay for child care. The small restaurant that Betty had worked in during summer vacations offered Betty a job and it was within walking distance, so she wouldn't have many expenses until she got her own place.

Late one night Annette was startled from her slumber by a hand on her arm. She looked up to find Betty. Her skin looked about one shade away from color of wite-out. "Betty, what's wrong? Are you okay?"

"I don't know, Annette. I just don't feel right. Maybe it's indigestion or something."

"It very well could be. Well, let's go back to your room and you can lie down. I don't want to wake up Joshua unless we have to," Annette reasoned.

Annette had Betty lay on her side. Within a couple of minutes, she began to groan. "I'm feeling that weird feeling again." Annette put a hand on Betty's abdomen, which was rising and felt hard. "Betty, you're having contractions," she told her.

Betty looked surprised. "They don't hurt all that bad."

"Oh, they'll get a lot worse before it's all over with," Annette told her, thinking about all of the OB patients she'd helped take care of.

"Do we have to go to the hospital now?" Betty asked.

"No, we'll wait and make sure they're getting closer together to be sure this is the real thing and not false labor," Annette told her.

"I'm glad someone knows what's going on," Betty pouted.

Over the next couple of hours, the contractions quickly went from fifteen minutes apart, to ten. When the first ones started coming every seven minutes apart, Annette decided it was time to go to the hospital.

Annette woke her husband and let him know what was going on. "Should I come to the hospital?" he asked.

"Nah, you can stay here and get some rest. You can come in the morning. With it being her first baby she probably won't have the baby until then, and you'll be bored sitting around waiting in the wee hours of the morning when you could be home resting."

"Okay, honey. Whatever you think is best. You're the nurse," he looked up with his heavy eyes and gave his wife a sleepy smile. She reached down and ruffled his hair.

Annette quickly got dressed and was putting her hair back in a ponytail when she heard Betty let out a loud yelp from the living room. Annette ran up to her and found Betty bent over, grasping her abdomen.

"Betty, are you okay?"

"Yeah, I'm fine, Annette. It's eased up now. But that one was REALLY bad."

Annette noticed water trickling down Betty's legs. She grabbed some towels from the hall closet to attempt to save her car interior, and rushed Betty into the car.

When the girls arrived, Annette was relieved to find a good friend of hers, Araya, working in OB that night. She felt much more comfortable having someone she trusted to care for her friend, especially since Betty was not handling her labor too well by this time.

After getting her registered, Annette was at Betty's side, trying to talk her through the breathing exercises they had learned in the Lamaze classes Annette signed her up for. "This stupid breathing stuff isn't working, Annette. I need some *medicine,*" Betty whined as the contractions intensified.

Dr Franklin was on call that night for OB. Annette didn't know him all that well, but had worked with him a few times. He saw that Betty was 4 centimeters dilated and told her she could have an epidural if she wanted. Betty accepted it with no hesitation at all.

Once the epidural was in effect, Betty was a different person. She was smiling, laughing, and joking around. "Annette, when you have a baby, make sure you get one of these as soon as the pregnancy test comes back positive," she told her friend, who groaned and rolled her eyes at the unoriginal joke.

While Betty was feeling comfortable, she took a nap and Annette took advantage of that and took one herself. Araya woke them up when she came into the room to check Betty, since the baby's heart rate was dropping with contractions.

The nurse told Betty "You're fully dilated, and I'm going to get the doctor, so hang tight."

Araya had been gone a few minutes when Betty told Annette she was feeling a lot of pressure and was getting the urge to push.

"Please don't push, Betty, the doctor will be in here in just a minute," Annette coaxed. "Pant and blow out like you're trying to blow out candles on a birthday cake."

"I'm trying, but it's not helping. I have to push!"

"No, Betty, please don't. I don't want to deliver any babies on my day off."

Dr. Franklin walked in, not a moment too soon. The new baby boy was born just minutes after he got his gown and gloves on.

Annette looked down at the tiny, crying infant. He had just returned from being weighted, bathed, and examined in the nursery. He was so small and pink, with deep blue eyes and a small tuft of soft dark hair right on the top of his head. Annette put her finger in the baby's tiny hand, and he curled his fingers around her and seemed to look into her eyes.

Annette had helped deliver dozens of babies, but she didn't remember ever seeing one as beautiful as this one. He was a petite six pounds, but was absolutely perfect.

She told Betty, "He is beautiful. You did a great job. But you know, you have to decide on a name for him now."

Betty moaned. "I know, I went through that baby name book a dozen times, but I just couldn't seem to settle on a name I really liked for a boy. What do you think I should name him? Help me pick something, Annette, please?"

"Jacob. He definitely looks like a Jacob to me," Annette surprised herself by saying that. Until that moment, she had been planning to save that name for her own son one day. Somehow right then, she changed her mind and felt like this baby should have it.

"He does kinda look like a Jacob! Okay, Jacob it is," Betty looked down at the baby. "You are good at this baby naming stuff. It almost seemed like you had his name already picked out."

"I suppose I had, in a way," Annette answered. She decided not to tell Betty she had picked out that name for her own child. She didn't want her friend to feel bad about "taking" her baby name.

"Can they take the baby back to the nursery now? I'm really tired. I feel like I ran a marathon. Guess they really don't call it 'labor' for nothing," Betty smiled weakly.

"I'll hold him for a while, Betty. You just rest," Annette took the baby in her arms. He snuggled into the crook of her elbow and fell quickly to sleep. Looking at the sweet sleeping infant, Annette realized that she wanted a baby of her own more than ever.

CHAPTER ELEVEN- NEW BEGINNINGS

After a couple of days in the hospital, little Jacob came home with Betty, Annette, and Joshua. Annette tried to encourage Betty to breastfeed. She cited the many health advantages for the baby as well as a reduction in the formula that Annette and Joshua were paying for. After a few days Betty decided that breastfeeding was too hard and gave up on it.

Annette stayed out of work for two weeks with Betty and the baby. Betty took full advantage of that. She slept late every morning. When the baby woke up hungry early in the morning, Annette often found Betty with a pillow over her head, trying to muffle the cries. Annette would usually grab the baby and make his bottle herself.

Annette really didn't mind taking care of Jacob. In fact, she loved it. She always had loved babies, and Jacob held a special place in her heart. She just thought Betty should take responsibility for caring for her own child. Plus, Annette would not always be there to help when Betty got a job and moved out on her own.

The first few days, Annette didn't complain. She knew that Betty was recovering from childbirth and needed rest to recuperate. As the two weeks of vacation time came to an end, though, she realized Betty was going to have to start caring for the baby herself. One night, at her wit's end after having a long day, she decided to pray.

"Lord, I'm trying to be patient with Betty, I really am, but sometimes it feels like she's taking advantage of me. I'm doing so much for her. I know that she's in a situation she wasn't prepared for, but my patience is running low with her lately. Please help me be strong, for baby Jacob's sake. Amen."

Annette sat Betty down to have a serious talk with her a few days before she was due to go back to work. She told her all of these concerns. Betty broke down and started to cry.

"You just don't realize how hard it is for me. He cries all the time! I'm still recovering from giving birth, learning to take care of him, and I don't have anybody around for me. You have Joshua!

Jacob's father Alex could care less that he's a daddy. I even called his mom to tell her about the baby and she said Alex told her the baby wasn't his and not to believe a word that I said. Do you have any idea how much that hurts?

And to make it all worse, I have to see you and Joshua

together, so happy and in love…" Betty sobbed uncontrollably and Annette went to her, held her in her arms, and stroked her hair softly.

"I know it's hard, sweetie, but I'm going back to work in a few days. You're going to be on your own. You're going to have to learn to take care of Jacob by yourself.

I'm trying really hard to be patient and help you until you move out, but to be honest with you, my patience is wearing thin, Betty. I do sympathize with you, but you are Jacob's mother and it's time for you to start acting like it.

I'm telling you all of this as your friend, Betty. You may think that I'm being tough on you, but you need to hear this. I'm saying all of it out of love."

Annette shuddered to think of what would have happened to Betty and Jacob if she hadn't taken them in. They could have ended up out on the streets. Annette hoped this realization would wake Betty up and make her take more responsibility when it came to taking care of her son.

* * *

Any improvements Betty made were minimal and short-lived. A few days later she was back to her old ways, and a worried Annette had to go back to work. Her first day back, Annette opened the front door and could hear Jacob's screaming in the spare bedroom. Betty was asleep on the couch, the sofa cushion pressed over her ear.

Annette was steaming as she walked over to her. "Betty, wake up! Your child is crying," she snapped.

Betty moaned, "That's all he's been doing *all* day. I'm so *tired*. Nothing I do makes him happy anyway."

Annette heaved a great sigh and went to the bedroom to comfort little Jacob. As soon as she picked him up, his sobs settled down. She changed his diaper which was soaked, and Jacob curled his little body against her shoulder and fell asleep. Annette felt his soft breath against her cheek, and suddenly felt a longing in her heart.

"Why can't he be mine?" She softly asked God. "Betty's not taking care of him, and it hurts so bad to love this baby so much and watch his mother not take care of him. But what am I supposed to do? If I kick Betty out, Jacob is going to suffer, and I can't bring myself to do that. Lord, please, just let me know what I need to do."

Annette had a more serious talk with Betty that night, and told her that she had no choice. She had to straighten out and care for her child like he needed to be, or they would have to find somewhere else to live. Annette had a feeling Betty knew she didn't have the heart to leave them with nowhere to live, but she had to find a way to get through to her. As hard as she tried to be patient, she felt herself losing her temper far too often. Annette was usually very even-tempered and she felt like she was becoming a person that she didn't want to be.

The following day after work, Annette came home hoping she wouldn't walk into a repeat of the day before. Instead she had a surprise awaiting her.

The house was silent. At first Annette figured that Betty and the baby were both asleep in the spare bedroom. "Betty?" she called out as she went from room to room. There was no trace of them.

Jacob's diaper bag, diapers, and formula were gone, but Annette knew Betty couldn't have gotten far without money. *Unless...* Annette went to the dresser where she kept a ceramic jar that held her emergency money that she never touched. The jar was empty.

Annette slumped to the floor, sobbing. Betty must have gotten mad at her for being so tough on her, and she had taken Jacob away. She cried for Jacob, not knowing what would happen to him. She cried for Betty, her best friend at one time who had now completely changed, and she cried for herself. She loved Jacob and wanted him there with her even though she knew he wasn't hers.

The shrill ring of the phone made Annette jump. She ran to it. "Betty?"

"No, dear. It's your mom."

"Mommy!" Annette cried out like a two year old. She took a breath and tried to gain enough composure to tell her mom what happened. "Betty left, and she took Jacob with her."

"No, she didn't, hon. Jacob is here. Betty took a cab over here around noon. I don't know where she got the money from.

Anyhow, she said she had something she needed to do. She hasn't come back yet, and I don't know when or if she will. There's a letter in Jacob's diaper bag addressed to you. We didn't open it since it had your name on it. I don't know what it says."

"I'm on my way, mom. If Betty gets there before I do, please try to talk her out of leaving with the baby." Annette hung up the phone, grabbed her keys, and headed for the door.

When she arrived at her parents' house, Annette immediately took Jacob from her mother's arms and showered his tiny face with kisses. "I'm so glad your mommy didn't take you away. I would have missed you so much," Jacob just stretched and yawned, his eyes heavy.

"Speaking of his mommy…" Annette's mom went over to the countertop and grabbed the envelope with Annette's name on it. She handed it to her daughter. Mrs. Wilkins and Alisa hovered around her. Annette could tell that they were anxious to find out what the letter said.

"Can you take the baby for just a few minutes, mom? I'd like to read this letter in private."

"I'll take him," Alisa offered. She cradled the infant in her arms. "Mom was waiting on you to get here so she could start dinner so I'll hold him while you do that."

"Thanks, Alisa." Annette went to her old bedroom. Her parents had talked about changing it into an office or a workout room, but so far it was still the same.

She made herself comfortable on the familiar old bed and opened the envelope. She began to read:

Dear Annette

I know I've let you down in so many ways. It was so irresponsible for me to get pregnant, and I know that I'm nowhere near being ready to take care of someone else. I can barely take care of myself.

When I got pregnant, I thought about giving the baby up for adoption. I never told anyone, though, because I thought everyone would think that I was a bad person. And I thought that maybe once I had the baby everything would change.

Last night I did a lot of hard thinking about everything you had said to me all the times we had our long conversations. I decided that you would make a better mom for Jacob than me. I know you love him more than anything and you will take good care of him.

I'm going back to New York. I called an agent who is going to get me some acting and modeling jobs once I lose my last few pounds from having the baby. I'm going to stay with a friend of mine from school. I'm still determined to do something with my life, and it's not raising babies. At least, not for now.

I will call you after I get settled in the city. Just let me know what I need to do or sign to make the adoption legal. I love you and please give Jacob a kiss for me every night. I know it seems selfish, but he'll be much better off without me.

Love, Betty

Annette collapsed onto her pillow, which absorbed her falling tears. She felt such anger and pity for Betty at the same time. She couldn't understand how someone could leave their child, even if it *was* with a dear friend. On the other hand, she agreed that Betty was not responsible enough to care for Jacob at this time.

After recuperating for a while, Annette found Alisa and Jacob in the living room. Although she was stunned at this turn of events, a part of Annette's heart leapt. The baby that she loved so dearly was going to be hers to keep, forever.

CHAPTER TWELVE- TRULY MEANT TO BE

For once, Betty kept her promise to Annette. She came to court when she was scheduled to go to finalize the adoption process. Before court came into session, Annette went up to Betty to show her a photograph of Jacob.

"I can't believe how big he's gotten! Look at all the hair he's gotten! And the chubby cheeks, just make you want to pinch them," Betty laughed.

"Would you like to come see him after we get done here?" Annette asked.

"No, I think it's best that I didn't," Betty sighed. "I know that I made the right choice leaving him with you. But I'd like to write a letter for you to give him for when he's old enough to understand my reasons for doing this.

I want him to know I wasn't abandoning him. I was giving him a better life than I ever could on my own. You and Joshua are the parents I wish I had growing up. I know Jacob will be happy with you, and with any brothers or sisters you have for him."

"No, that's not going to happen, Betty," Annette said softly, looking down.

"Why not, Annette? I thought you and Joshua always wanted to have lots of children? I'm sure Jacob is a handful now, but maybe when he's a little older…"

"It's not that, Betty. Joshua and I never did anything to prevent me becoming pregnant. Then after we got Jacob, and Joshua got out of school and started making a good salary, we figured we'd have a baby of our own.

I was working part time anyway to spend time with Jacob, we figured it would be great to have both Jacob and the new baby home with me, and I would go back to working full time after they were both in kindergarten."

"That sounds like a great plan," Betty agreed. "Why did you change your mind?"

"I didn't. After several months of trying, I talked to Dr. Franklin. He said he was sure everything was okay and that it sometimes just takes a little time, but he decided to run some tests just to be sure.

He didn't expect to find anything wrong, but he did. That's how they found out. I had a tumor on my uterus.

Not only would I never be able to get pregnant or carry a baby on my own, but I also had to have a hysterectomy. It's a good thing I went to see him. Otherwise, it could have spread. Not having a baby could have been the least of my worries."

"Oh, Annette," Betty hugged her friend.

"It's okay. It was found in time and the doctor said he got all of it. It could have been much worse. Having Jacob helped me so much. Without him, the news would have been so much more devastating. We could have adopted, but that takes so long, and is so expensive, and it's rare to even get a baby…"

"Don't you see, Annette?" Betty asked. This was God's plan. My mistake wasn't a mistake at all. Jacob was meant to be yours from the beginning.

Now you're the wife and mother you always wanted to be, and I'm back in New York getting some modeling and acting jobs. Everything worked out for us. It wasn't the way we planned them. It was the way God planned them for us."

Annette stood there, stunned as she thought about what Betty said. She thought back to when she gave Jacob the name she'd always planned to give her own son. She thought about the longing she'd felt for Jacob when she held him, wishing he was her own, even though it felt wrong to wish that.

Betty had a child she couldn't care for, and Annette desperately wanted a child and couldn't have one. She didn't have Jacob the way she'd planned to have a child, but she knew she couldn't love him any more if she had. Jacob *was* her gift from God.

She reminded herself of that fact often as she watched Jacob grow up to become a wonderful young man. He always knew that he was adopted, but when he graduated from high school, with plans to start pre-med classes in the fall, Annette sat him down, gave him the note Betty wrote that day, and told him the story of how he was truly a gift from God.

EPILOGUE-
THE START
OF A NEW
LIFE

Jessica inked the last few words of her story, then chewed the end of her pen with a look of contentment on her face. She was happy with how her story had turned out. It was an important story to her, in more ways than one.

Jessica heard her mother stumbling in through the door. She rushed out to the living room to help her mom, who had obviously had quite a bit to drink. The man she was dating—at least for this week—looked Jessica up and down in a way that left her feeling a bit unsettled. The young girl closed her fuzzy secondhand robe tightly around her to cover her nightgown before taking her mother's arm.

"I will help her to bed, thanks. You can go now," she told the man whose name she wasn't sure of—Billy or Bobby maybe?

"Okay, suit yourself," Billy/Bobby shrugged his shoulders and spun around to leave, slamming the door as he went.

"Come on, mom, let's get you to bed." Jessica helped her mom to her bedroom. By the time she pulled the covers tightly up to her mother's chin, she could hear loud snoring. "Sleep tight, mom," Jessica said before turning to leave.

Jessica went back to own room and looked over the story she had just written. She daydreamed for a minute about having the kind of life that Annette had, the kind of life that she could have had if her circumstances had been different. She looked at the picture on her nightstand of her Aunt Annette who lived thousands of miles away. She was holding her little boy, and both of them looked at the camera with huge grins.

Jessica planned to take her book and type it, little by little, on the computers at school between classes and even on her lunch break if she had to.

Writing the book had been healing to her. Annette was who she had always wanted to be. In her writing she could create a character with the life she had always wanted. But although she knew it was too late to change the circumstances she was born into, it was not too late for her to follow a different path than her mother had.

She had decided she was going to make something of her life, no matter what kind of situation she was stuck in—and writing this book was the first step.